For my three little helpers, Kate, Jane, and Mr. Teddy Underfoot —DM

*For Emma, Molly, and all the moms who make it work
each and every day —CD*

ABOUT THIS BOOK

The illustrations for this book were done in digital chalk. This book was edited by Nikki Garcia and designed by Patrick Collins with art direction from Saho Fujii. The production was supervised by Kimberly Stella, and the production editor was Jen Graham. The text was set in Just Tell Me What, and the display type is Chauncy Decaf.

Little, Brown and Company • Hachette Book Group • 1290 Avenue of the Americas, New York, NY 10104 • Visit us at LBYR.com • First Edition: September 2021 • Little, Brown and Company is a division of Hachette Book Group, Inc. • The Little, Brown name and logo are trademarks of Hachette Book Group, Inc. • The publisher is not responsible for websites (or their content) that are not owned by the publisher. • Library of Congress Cataloging-in-Publication Data • Names: Murray, Diana, author. | Doerrfeld, Cori, illustrator. • Title: Help Mom work from home! / by Diana Murray ; illustrated by Cori Doerrfeld. • Description: First edition. | New York ; Boston : Little, Brown and Company, 2021. | Audience: Ages 4–8. | Summary: "A mom and her child spend a day together working from home." —Provided by publisher. • Identifiers: LCCN 2020055623 | ISBN 9780316273657 (hardcover) • Subjects: CYAC: Stories in rhyme. | Mother and child—Fiction. | Work—Fiction. | Humorous stories. • Classification: LCC PZ8.3.M9362 He 2021 | DDC [E]—dc23 • LC record available at https://lccn.loc.gov/2020055623 • ISBN 978-0-316-27365-7 • PRINTED IN CHINA • APS • 10 9 8 7 6 5 4 3 2 1

HELP MOM WORK FROM HOME!

Diana Murray

Illustrated by Cori Doerrfeld

L B
LITTLE, BROWN AND COMPANY
New York   Boston

Home is a great place
to sit and relax,
to read and play games,
or to munch lots of snacks.

Plus, home is so cozy,
so quiet and calm,
it's a great place to work!
Both for *you* and *your mom*!

With your bold can-do spirit,
your spunk and your speed,

you're a natural boss!
You can help Mom **succeed!**

What's first on your list?
She must look like a pro!
Help her dress to impress.
Do her hair up, just so.

Next you can gather important supplies.

Line them up neatly according to size.

Arrange all the pencils
and pens that Mom has,
and show her how crayons
add extra pizzazz!

Bedazzle some business cards.
Hang snazzy signs.
A few drops of glitter…

...and **everything shines!**

Have meetings, take notes,

make some calls, be persistent.

For even *more* help...

...you can hire **an assistant!**

If Mom's looking frazzled,
she might need a break.

Make her some tea
and your fanciest cake!

Show her a few
of your yoga moves, too.

After some stretches,
she'll feel good as new.

When break time has ended,
you'll get back to stacking,

stamping and sorting,
and busily packing,

making deliveries,

labeling folders,

and checking Mom's work,
peeking over her shoulders.

When the workday is over,
count up all the pay.

Hand Mom a gold star
for her hard work today.

Then point out the progress
she's made on your chart.
There's lots more to plan,
but this marks a good start!

It's time to go home...
but you're already there!

Give Mom that **big bonus** you wanted to share.

And then one last phone call:
You've both **earned a treat!**

Order some takeout
and put up your feet.

When you're working from home,
there is so much to do,
and nobody else
can help Mom quite like you!

Sunday	Monday	Tuesday	Wedn
4	5 • video chat with Grandma	6	7
11 • build a fort	12	13	14
18	19 • dance party	20	21
25	26	27 • go to lake	28

INVOICE